SILAS
THE BOOKSTORE CAT

KAREN TRELLA MATHER

ILLUSTRATED BY CHRIS VAN DUSEN

DOWN EAST BOOKS
CAMDEN, MAINE

Story copyright © 1994 by Karen Trella Mather

Illustrations © 1994 by Chris Van Dusen

ISBN 0-89272-352-1

Library of Congress Catalog Card Number 94-72357

Cover design by Tim Seymour Designs

Color separations and printing by Piguet Graphics and
Everbest Printing, Hong Kong, through Four Colour Imports,
Louisville, KY.

4   2   5   3   1

Down East Books / Camden, Maine

There are all sorts of cats just as there are all sorts of people. There are finicky cats that turn their heads away from anyone or anything that does not suit them. There are alley cats that only like other cats. But there are also cats that love to be around people and care for them. Silas was just such a cat. He loved the people who came into his bookstore.

Silas knew exactly what he was expected to do around the store.

He complimented customers on the books they chose.

He allowed children to pet him, if they were quiet and gentle.

He helped display the books on the sale table,

and he kept the basement, where his food bowl and litter box were,
clean of mice.

Of course, it was also necessary to inspect whatever work Mr. Snow and Mrs. Wheeler might be doing. They were the store owners and were always busy. New books came in big boxes, and Silas was always ready to help unpack them. He would jump into the boxes and scratch through the packing material to make sure the boxes were empty.

After Silas finished sniffing and shredding the paper inside the boxes, he always had a ready-made, cozy place for a quick nap.

It was after just such a nap on a quiet afternoon that Silas stretched and took a stroll. First he went into the children's section and sniffed the big pillows on the floor where children could sit and read. One pillow was very lumpy, and Silas gave it a good kneading with his front paws.

Then he noticed a man placing fresh newspapers in the racks by the front door.

Silas decided he would check out the front page to see what was happening in the world. Looking around to make sure no customers needed his help just then, Silas hopped into the middle bin and fell asleep.

As Silas lay asleep, the front door whisked open beside him. In stepped a mother pulling her son by the cuff of his jacket. "Just pick out a book, Peter. They have a whole rack of interesting books in this store. Remember, your teacher said to read a book every week."

Peter kept his head down inside the hood of his jacket. He pulled against his mother, trying to get back out the door. "But I don't want to come in, and I don't want a stupid book! They're boring! I could be playing soccer right now with John and Michael at the park!"

Silas lifted his head and yawned, curling his pink sandpaper tongue. He watched as Peter stopped at the first display table, where there were some books stacked in a pyramid. Peter stood on his toes and stretched out his arm. He could just reach the top book. He grabbed it without even looking at it, then held it out to his mother.

"Here, then I'll take this one," he said. "Now let's go to the park."

Peter's mother firmly shook her head. "That is an adult book on how to plan a wedding. It is certainly not a subject that would interest you. Now stop this silliness, and let's go look at the books in the children's section."

Peter stood on tiptoe again to return the book to the top of the pyramid stack. He was thinking that his mother did not understand. There was no such thing as an interesting book. Reading was just something you had to do for school.

As he put the book back on the top of the stack, he gave it an angry shove. *Crash! Ka-boom!* The whole big pyramid of books tumbled off the table and down to the floor.

Peter's mother whirled around so fast that her pocketbook swung out from her arm like a slingshot, nearly knocking over another customer. Mr. Snow was so startled, he almost shut the cash register on his thumb. Poor Silas jumped off the newspaper bin and hid behind it, the fur on his back frizzing up like porcupine quills.

"I'm sorry! It was an accident," Peter said quickly.

His mother frowned and put her hands on her hips. "Well, accident or not, this mess needs to be picked up. Put all the books back just as they were while I go to the children's section and pick out your book for this week."

Peter began to put the books back on the table. It really wasn't his fault, he thought. If only his mother hadn't insisted on bringing him here in the first place, none of this would have happened.

Then Peter was nudged from behind. He turned and was so surprised to see a big white cat rubbing against him that he almost dropped another book. "Wow! Hi, fella! You look like a snow cat. I bet you'd rather be outside, too. You don't have to read any dumb books."

Silas rolled on his back and showed his white tummy. He blinked his grape-green eyes and looked up at Peter in a friendly way.

Peter quickly finished picking up all the books. The big white cat was more fun than any book. "Here, boy. Here, boy," Peter called. He pounced on Silas and swooped him up in his arms. "You can stay with me until my mom is done shopping."

But Silas did not think this was a good idea. Silas did not like to be picked up at all. It was a scary feeling being held around the middle, with his back feet dangling down toward the floor below.

With a frightened *Me-ooow*, Silas scrambled with his back paws, then pushed off against Peter's stomach. As soon as his feet hit the floor, Silas darted down a side aisle, as fast as he could go.

"Hey! Wait for me!" Peter hurried down the same aisle. But where was Silas? There were bookshelves on both sides, but no space for a cat to hide under. He saw Mrs. Wheeler nearby, putting new books on the shelves.

"Excuse me, do you know where the big white cat is?" he asked.

Mrs. Wheeler looked up from the books and smiled. "His name is Silas. Check in the back. I believe I saw him there earlier."

Peter walked toward the back of the store. He passed racks of
calendars, cards, and gifts, but, most of all, he passed shelves filled with
books. Peter was surprised to see so many different pictures on the book
covers. One showed a man climbing a mountain. Another showed a baby
with a silly hat. On a third, a smiling woman held up pies. There were so
many books about so many things. Peter wondered if they would all be
taken home and read. That would be a lot of reading!

Finally, Peter spotted Silas on the copy machine and ran over to pet him.

Silas cautiously sat up and stretched. He liked it when Peter rubbed the ruff of fur around his neck, but he was still afraid Peter might try to pick him up again.

Silas twitched his tail, tickling Peter under the nose and making him laugh.

Peter's mother came over. He could see that she had a book tucked under one arm. She held it up for him to see. "Look what I found on dinosaur bones. Remember how well you did with that other dinosaur book we have at home?"

Peter frowned. "It was okay. But I could only read parts of it. You had to help with the rest."

His mother smiled and ruffled Peter's hair. "But Peter, no one learns to read in one day. Reading takes practice too, just like soccer or baseball. Think of it this way—reading is a gift, but not one that can be given all at once. Some words you'll already know, but the best words will be the new words you'll learn."

Peter did not say anything. He was thinking, what did words matter when the stories never interested him anyway? "But, Mom, I don't want to read about dinosaurs anymore. I liked them *last* year."

Peter's mother looked at her watch. "We have to leave in fifteen minutes. I'll go back to the children's section. But, if you don't come to choose a book you *do* like, then dinosaurs it will be."

Silas settled back down on the warm copy machine. Peter was petting him gently, just how he liked, behind the ears. But as soon as Peter's mother left, Silas saw a mischievous twinkle in Peter's eyes. "Forget the book, Silas. Let's play tag again."

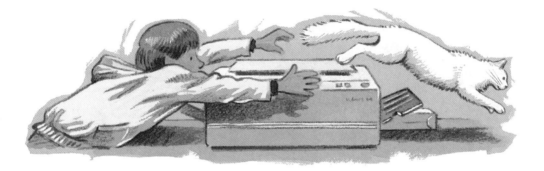

Uh-oh! Silas knew what was coming next. Peter made a grab for Silas, but Silas had already jumped off the copier and was running toward a display table covered with a long cloth that hung to the floor. In a second, Silas had scooted under the cloth.

Peter crouched on his hands and knees and lifted the tablecloth edge. In the darkness, he could see Silas's eyes glowing, but the cat was too far back to be reached.

Peter sat back and sighed, "No one wants me to have any fun."

Mrs. Wheeler came from behind the counter and stood next to Peter. "Silas likes you, Peter. He just doesn't want to be picked up or chased. What he really likes is for someone to sit quietly. Then, he will come to *you*. Why don't you find a book and sit there?" Mrs. Wheeler pointed to the floor pillows in the children's section.

After Mrs. Wheeler left, Peter looked under the table again. Silas was still there, staring back. "Gee, Silas, I didn't mean to scare you. I'll be over here, okay?"

But Silas only stared some more.

Peter stood up. The only thing left to do was sit down with a book, like Mrs. Wheeler had said. Then, maybe, Silas would come out of his hiding place. Peter started looking at the books on the display table. To his surprise, there was a picture of a football player on one of them. The book was called, *Kick, Pass, and Run,* by Leonard Kessler. A whole book about football? Now that might not be so bad.

Peter walked around the table—slowly this time—to see what other books were there. Then he stopped. His eyes grew big. There it was! The perfect book! Peter hurried to show the book to his mother.

A few minutes later, Silas came out to look for Peter. Where had he gone?

Then he heard Peter say, "Hey, Mom, this is it—the perfect book!"

Silas walked over to the children's section and found Peter with his
mother. Peter grinned when he saw Silas, but, this time he held onto his
book instead of grabbing for the cat. "Hi, Silas. I was hoping you'd come out.
I've got something to show you."

Then Peter showed Silas what he was holding. It was a book about Peter's

favorite sport, soccer. Its title was *Super Soccer Sunday.* Peter and his mother laughed as Silas politely sniffed the cover, then rubbed against Peter's leg.

Silas followed Peter and his mother to the register, where they paid for Peter's new book. Peter knelt down to scratch behind Silas's ears. "Too bad cats can't really learn to read. But don't worry, Silas. I can always come and read to you instead."

Silas yawned. It had been a busy day. He jumped into his favorite newspaper bin by the door. He curled his body into a comfortable ball and closed his eyes. Then Silas dreamed a little dream that all the words in all the books in the bookstore suddenly made sense to him.

Of course, he had a favorite story. It was called *The Cat Who Learned to Read.*

Silas, the Bookstore Cat was inspired by a real cat named Silas, who has been entertaining customers in a small Maine bookstore for the past ten years. Abandoned as a kitten by his original owner, Silas was discovered one winter afternoon by a kind woman who let him into her apartment. It soon became clear that her other cats would not allow Silas to stay, so she looked for another home for him. She decided to ask the manager and owner of the bookstore where she worked if it would be possible to add one white cat to the bookstore staff.

They said yes, and to everyone's delight, the young cat became an immediate attraction. He befriended customers of all ages—especially children—with his elegance, charm, and quiet good nature. The bookstore staff named him Silas, after *Silas Marner*.

In 1992, a photographer happened to see Silas sitting in the bookstore window, and this led to a feature article about Silas in the December 1992 issue of the Italian magazine *Quattrozampe*. Silas was later featured as a "Remarkable Cat" in *Cats Magazine*'s January 1993 issue, inspiring fan mail from as far away as Alaska.

Unspoiled by such fame and attention. Silas still resides at the bookstore, doing what he does best: being an outstanding bookstore cat.